# WORLDS APART

## Short Story Anthology

K. Morral

authorHOUSE

*AuthorHouse™ UK*
*1663 Liberty Drive*
*Bloomington, IN 47403 USA*
*www.authorhouse.co.uk*
*Phone: 0800.197.4150*

*© 2016 K. Morral. All rights reserved.*

*No part of this book may be reproduced, stored in a retrieval system, or transmitted by any means without the written permission of the author.*

*Published by AuthorHouse 11/07/2016*

*ISBN: 978-1-5246-6569-2 (sc)*
*ISBN: 978-1-5246-6570-8 (e)*

*Print information available on the last page.*

*Any people depicted in stock imagery provided by Thinkstock are models, and such images are being used for illustrative purposes only.*
*Certain stock imagery © Thinkstock.*

*This book is printed on acid-free paper.*

*Because of the dynamic nature of the Internet, any web addresses or links contained in this book may have changed since publication and may no longer be valid. The views expressed in this work are solely those of the author and do not necessarily reflect the views of the publisher, and the publisher hereby disclaims any responsibility for them.*

# Table of Contents

Halloween Horror ................................................................. 1
Justice ................................................................................ 11
Anniversary on the Canal ............................................... 15
Into the Deep ..................................................................... 20
Resolution ......................................................................... 31
Revelations ....................................................................... 46

I have been a keen reader and writer of fantasy fiction for many years. They draw me into a different world, share experiences that I may never otherwise have in my rather ordinary life. This anthology is my way of extending my absorption to other readers.

Place is very important to me. It is where we experience our own lives, where we love, hate, relax, or even cry with friends, and family. In my stories I try to create places that everyone can relate to, that enables readers to locate my characters and actions and to connect them to the world they inhabit. I revel in writing to relate to all the senses to conjure up settings readers can see, feel, hear and even smell.

Each of the six stories in this collection explores the emotions of the main characters, drawing the reader into an episode of their lives as they face challenges and battle with themselves, with history or with global perceptions to find a conclusion to their problems.

No story is set in the same place. From a gloomy backstreet or a dilapidated living room to a bright Caribbean island or a Welsh quarry, the stories use the setting to provide a vibrant context in which the drama unfolds.

Halloween Horror explores a supernatural return home from an evening out, while Justice gives a brief insight into the lives of occupants in a forgotten part of a city. Anniversary on the canal shares a foggy October evening with an occupant of a canal boat living through the horror of her own memories. Into the Deep gives the reader the opportunity to escape as the main character seeks to resolve her own conflicts. Resolution follows a daughter seeking to find ways to help her mother move on, whilst Revelations sees a team building exercise go very wrong and forces the boss to expose more of herself than ever intended.

# Halloween Horror

"People are so gullible!" Paul scoffed. "I can't believe that they actually buy this stuff!"
"Well, it shows that we're good at our job!" Lynette sniffed, lifting her long skirts to step over a puddle.
"Yes, but the reason that we have this job in the first place is that idiots actually believe in ghosts!"
Pausing, he studied their reflections in a shop window. Lynette's oval face gazed back at him, eyes anxiously darting along the street. Foundation paled skin and dark circles around her eye were framed by the shadows of her dark hood. Her normally thin lips were plush with dark purple lipstick as wisps of dark hair straggled across her cheeks, escaped from her concealed bun. The hood flowed over her shoulders and into the cloak that floated in the breeze.
Shifting his gaze, he examined his own reflection. His top hat rested on a pale forehead above similarly darkened eyes and lips. A thick line of dark red 'blood' was visible just above the line of his collar. Something flickered in the glass, to the left of his reflection. He frowned. It seemed to be the image of a man watching them, but glancing over his shoulder he saw no one.

"Come on. It's cold." Lynette shivered.

She glanced around, unwilling to voice her disquiet, but eager to leave the silence of the street. She hadn't been keen to work Halloween, but the money had been too good to refuse.

Nodding, Paul turned and they continued, habitually striding along to the click of Paul's cane on the pavement. Lynette relaxed as the bulky presence of their boss became visible in the doorway. He always liked to count them in.

"Good night?" Malcolm grunted, looking past them down the street.

"Yeah." Paul nodded.

Chuckling, he thought back to the group of American tourists who had been so scared that they left the cemetery at a run. "The fools didn't see any of it coming."

"Good. Glad you made it back alright. Go on in and change. We're just waiting for Michael and Rose."

"But they left the graveyard before us!" Lynette gasped.

Malcolm turned to look at her and she noted the worried creases over his dark eyes.

"They're probably taking a moment to themselves!" Paul shook his head. "Couples do that sometimes. Come on."

Unconvinced, Lynette followed him down the narrow stairway to the basement. Turning into the male changing room, Paul noted Jim's skeleton hanging on the wall.

"Typical of him not to wait" he muttered to himself as he removed his top hat.

As he sat in front of the mirror he reached for the facial wipes to remove the thick make-up. He shivered in a sudden draft. The lights surrounding the mirror flickered, almost responding to the breeze as candle flames.

"Have your lights gone funny?" He turned and shouted to Lynette.

"No, but it has gone very cold!" Lynette's voice wavered. "Can we hurry up and go?"

"I'm trying!"

Turning back to the mirror, he lifted a wipe to his cheek and froze. His eyes settled on the flickering image of a man to the left of his reflection. He released a breath and scowled.

"Very funny Jim." Dropping the cloth to the table, he clapped slowly. "Yes, we all know you want this part. It'll be all yours when I leave this summer. You've clearly been working on the costume. That blood is damn good. How have you've got it to flow…" Spinning in his chair he gaped across an empty room.

Swallowing a sudden knot in his throat, he turned back to the mirror. Eyes wide, he watched, motionless, as a grin slowly spread across the pale face before him. Paul's gaze drifted to red stained collar of the man standing by his shoulder. Blood was pouring from a long gash across the throat. Transfixed, Paul's hand drifted to his own neck. His fingers skimmed the crusted line of paint. Gasping for breath, Paul flung himself backwards. The chair toppled to the floor.

"Paul, my zip is stuck. Can you help me get it loose?" Lynette asked, stepping into the room.

The man vanished. With his heart hammering in his chest, Paul glanced wildly about the small room.

"What?" he snapped at Lynette, turning back to stare at the empty mirror. Beads of sweat glistened across his forehead. He could feel the slow creep of a bead trail down his spine.

"I asked if you could help me ... What are you looking at?"

"Get your clothes." He ordered.

"But you're not... We're not..." Lynette gaped, unnerved by the wide-eyed demeanour of the normally calm Paul.

"I'm not staying here to wait for more of Jim's practical jokes!" Paul snarled, grabbing his coat.

He strode past her towards the stairs.

"You can either stay here and change alone or get your clothes and change at home!"

Lynette turned and raced to get her clothes. Paul took the stairs two at a time to get into the open.

"Malc?!" Stepping into the cold night air, he was surprised to find his boss had vanished.

"Where's Malc?" Lynette asked, panting as she joined him, clutching a bag to her chest.

"Probably in his office." Paul shrugged off a growing concern that was lodging itself in his mind. He couldn't get the image of the strange man's reflection out of his head. He shivered. There had been something malicious in his grin.

"Come on. We'll call him to tell him we're off."

"But what about…He didn't tell…" Lynette almost shrieked as nerves began to take a firmer hold.

Unable to answer Lynette's questions, Paul flipped open his phone. He hit the speed dial button and lifted the device to his ear. The ringing echoed between the phone at his ear and the phone in the office. The disjointed rhythm faded as he strode out into the street.

"Come on Malc! Pick up!" he cursed.

He ignored Lynette's whimper.

"Malcolm Seers Dark City Tours. Please leave a message."

"Damn it, Malc. Where are you? Just calling to let you know that Lynette and I have gone home. We'll bring back our costumes tomorrow. It's just got a bit … weird. Call me when you get this…Please." Paul flipped the phone closed before slipping it in his pocket.

"What's wrong Paul? What's happening?"

Paul glanced across at Lynette who was puffing alongside him as she held her skirts above her knees.

"I don't know."

They rushed through the streets as a cold mist descended on the city. Street lamps cast long shadows at every corner. Every so often, Paul would catch a glimpse of themselves in shop windows. The reflection of a man strode along side them, tapping his cane on the pavement. But whenever Paul glanced round, he saw no-one else. With each window, Paul increased his pace.

As the security gates of the campus came into view, Paul broke into a run. Lynette followed suit. Paul's long legs carried him forwards faster, and he soon pulled away from his companion.

A scream sliced through the mist. It pierced his fear. He stopped, turning back. His racing heart urged him to save himself. Lynette had vanished. Her bag lay crumpled on the pavement, the contents still settling across the ground. Gasping for breath, Paul stepped forwards. Wide eyed, he scanned the street. There was no one to see.

A movement caught his attention. Glancing to his left he stared into the dark confines of an unknown alley. The movement repeated; a soft billowing of fabric. Trying to swallow through his dry throat, he inched closer. A grey shadow stretched into the darkness. Heart hammering in his chest, he crept alongside. He found himself staring down at Lynette's lifeless body. With a cry, he dropped to his knees and reached out to stroke her pale cheek below eyes that stared blindly into nothing. It took him a few moments to realize that his knees were wet. Reaching down, he felt the sticky warmth of her still flowing lifeblood.

"Oh my God!" He pushed himself back, staggering into brickwork.

Breathing heavily, he stumbled into the street. He rushed up to the security guards office.

"Lynette...body...alley... blood..."he mumbled, gesturing wildly behind him.

Ignoring the startled glances of the guards, he didn't wait for a response. He had to get home. He was in danger. He didn't know what from, or why; he just knew that he was.

Fumbling with his keys, it took him several attempts to get the door to open. Falling into the house, he slammed the door shut. With legs trembling, he leaned against the door and took a deep breath. Sweat poured down his spine. Closing his eyes he sank down to the floor. The pounding of his heart vibrated through his body. Focusing on taking slow, deep breaths, he fought to gain control of himself. He was safe here.

"Did you really think a door would stop me?" A crackling voice spoke above him.

He opened his eyes with a start. He was staring at a pair of translucent legs alongside a slender black cane. He swallowed.

"No no no...."He closed his eyes tightly. "You can't... you're not... you can't be a..."

"I am many things and have been called many things. A doctor, a scientist, a psychopath, a murderer, evil are a few of the more common."

"You can't be ... here...!" Paul shouted, opening his eyes against his instincts.

"Why? Because I'm dead? You forget lad, it's Halloween! I couldn't resist paying a visit to the man who does me such flattery with his portrayal!"

"You can't...I must be imagining... No such thing..."

"So you keep telling yourself. Yet I would like to suggest otherwise." The spectre removed his hat and bowed slightly. "Jacob Smalley at your service." Replacing his hat, the spectre began to play with the knob at the top of his cane.

"What do you... why are you..."

"I thought that as you were doing such a good job of being me, it would be only fitting that you deserved a proper end!"

Paul stared mutely as a slender dagger was withdrawn from the cane. It glinted in the light as Jacob Smalley offered it to Paul to admire. Whimpering, Paul was transfixed by the line of metal. Jacob Smalley flicked his wrist. Whistling, the gleam of light flashed.

Flesh blood spurting towards him, the Jacob Smalley smiled. Dropping the blade across the outstretched knees, he faded into the netherworld.

### *Deadliest Halloween for 100 years*

*Six bodies have been found in Liverpool in the early hours of Saturday morning, the morning after Halloween, in scenes not dissimilar to gruesome discoveries made 100 years earlier.*

*The shocking discovery of 6 bodies around the city were trigged by the discovery of a female in 19$^{th}$ century costume following the return of a ghost tour actor to his student accommodation. Almost incoherent, the blood covered student, Paul Newman, mumbled wild descriptions to the guards at the security gate before fleeing. They discovered the girl lying in a side alley, surrounded in her own blood having been stabbed through the heart.*

*"We didn't know what to make of him at first." Says David, one the guards. "He was babbling insanely about some girls body. We didn't believe him until we found her."*

*After calling the police, the security guards followed the student to his flat to ensure the safety of others in the compound, only to find the door wedged shut. It was later discovered that the student's own body was leaning against the door, his throat cut by a rapier like blade by his side.*

*Later in the morning, the door to the ghost tour office was discovered open, and on further investigation the police found the bodies of the owner, and another student actor cut open. The owner had been spread across his desk, while the student actor was hanging from the pipes in the toilet, blood draining from his arm into the bowl of toilet.*

*As concern grew for the other members of the ghost tour, the bodies of two more student actors were discovered in bushes at St James Park, lying peacefully across the graves below the Anglican Cathedral.*

*All bodies bore identical wounds to those inflicted by Jacob Smalley, the psychopathic doctor and scientist portrayed on the ghost tour by Paul*

*Newman, the student who triggered the discoveries. Jacob Smalley operated in Liverpool at the turn of the century, and more than a hundred years ago on Halloween murdered five people with a slender rapier. His diary was discovered later, suggesting that the murders had been committed in the name of science, his attempt to collect the blood from different parts of the body for analysis.*

*When his evil activities were discovered, Jacob Smalley slit his own throat as he leaned against the door to his surgery in order to avoid a public hanging.*

*No motive is understood to have been discovered for the contemporary copycat killings, though no one else is thought to be involved. It is a worrying thought that in getting into his role, Paul Newman coldly murdered those around him 'in tribute' to the evil man he portrayed. Have we taken the ghost tour phenomenon a step too far by directly mirroring past events?*

Putting the newspaper down on the table, she reached for the scissors. It bore all the hallmarks of a visit. Each year there was an unexplained murder in Liverpool on Halloween, and every year she continued her search for means of destroying him. She had been too late for those poor souls, but she would continue for as long as necessary to put a halt to more meaningless murders.

# Justice

*Hiding in the shadows, she watches life as it plays out in the cobbled passages of her homeland. Observing the constant fight for survival that plagues everyone who lives in the forgotten backstreets of the city. Darkness is her friend, from where she observes, unnoticed and unknown, and from where she dispenses justice.*

That night, sounds of a struggle carried on the still, putrid air to her attentive ears. A sharp cry for help, whispered threats, thudding contact and rustling clothes suggested this is more than the usual drunken brawl. Through years of practice, Rosara slipped silently through the alleys. Gliding from shadow to shadow underneath the overhanging timber buildings, she avoided the flickering light from the few meagre candle street lamps.

Turning into a twitchel, barely wide enough for a horse and rider, her acute eyesight picked up a shaking bundle of rags in the darkness of a long disused doorway. The girl had wrapped her arms round her knees, burying her head to muffle her tears. Her sobs wracked her body, so she jerked and trembled whilst the scraps of clothing that hung loose from her shoulders danced.

Rosara could smell the lingering essence of fear. Blood continued to race underneath the ethereally pale skin, trying to steady after the ordeal. Such white skin was unusual in a part of the city where the residents wore dirt as another layer of protection from the permanent chill. Rosara paused a moment to take it in, delighting in the girls existence, despite her obvious fall from grace. There was still a world outside these streets.

Stepping forward, careful to announce her presence with the tap of her shoe on stone, Rosara crouched alongside the girl. Instantly, she was overwhelmed by the raw, acrid odour of terror. The girl tried to retreat further into the doorway, afraid of more rough treatment.

"Which way did they go?" Rosara whispered, careful to keep her face hidden.

She was the last, the only one willing to take responsibility for the sufferance of the residents. To serve the justice the few innocent folk desperately needed. What had started as a way of making amends for the sins of her kind had turned into a personal quest for salvation. Not just for herself, but also for the victims of the terrible atrocities that mankind could deliver upon weaker members of the same species. That would be lost if she was identified.

Trembling, the girl held out an arm that was more bone than flesh. Nodding, Rosara stood, turning to follow her directions over whelmed by an unusual despair. The girl had been beautiful once, had taken care of herself until fairly recently. What had driven her to the living hell of the Backstreets Rosara shuddered to think. For that torment to be furthered by a brutal gang rape.

Rosara could smell at least three men on the girl's drawn skin; had been able to see the red marks on her arms and shoulders lingering evidence of their 'caresses'. Rosara was certain that the girls face would be equally as marked.

Shaking her head at the cruelty, Rosara kept on her quest to find the perpetrators, but a thought crept into her head unbidden. The poor girl had miraculously survived, but her life would forever be a living hell. A daily fight for food and shelter, surviving on whatever could be scrounged, stolen or discovered. Living with the constant fear that the same or worse could happen again. Even if she learned that the three had met their justice, there would still be the fear that someone else; someone bigger, someone rougher. Would justice be better served by ridding the girl of that? Would it have been better if she had died?

Rosara shook her head, forcing herself to concentrate on the path ahead, and ignore the temptation to return to the girl. The thought often popped into her head after seeing the most tragic of victims, but she had no right to decide. She could dispense God's justice, but her punishment was such that she was unable to ease suffering.

She turned instinctively into an old arcade, a crumbling ruin of a once fancy shopping district. Empty bay windows projected and retreated into the central covered space, offering alcoves and private escapes to all who needed it. Pausing in the doorway, Rosara took a deep breath and sorted out the different scents that weighed heavy in the air.

A family of four, filthy and haggard, huddled in a corner under rotten blankets trying desperately to keep warm and survive the night. Further inside, a couple consummated some unimaginable passion, their lust as clear as their grunts that carried through the silence.

From the central depths of the arcade, Rosara could smell the three brutish men sated and relaxed as they shared a box bed as easily as they had shared the girl. To her satisfaction, she could hear their murmured thoughts as they used telepathy to communicate. There were few telepaths in the Backstreets.

The justice Rosara dispensed always meant death, but the level of suffering was always directly proportional to the crime. Rosara prided herself in that. And telepaths were very receptive to suffering.

Disregarding the claustrophobia that overwhelmed her mind when entering covered spaces, Rosara pressed forward into the silky darkness of the arcade. Tonight three people would learn of her existence. Three people would suffer the justice decided by their actions. Tonight, the last vampire would continue to assuage the guilt she carried for the rest of her kind. In driving out the good and the wealthy, they had turned the Backstreets into the very gates of hell.

# Anniversary on the Canal

MUFFLED IN HER WOOLLEN WRAP, Josie reached forward to add another log to the fire. The flames danced, crackling as they accepted her offering. Hinges creaked as she closed the metal door to the burner. Tucking her feet underneath her she turned to stare back out into the night. Darkness had descended rapidly, a thick blanket settling silence onto the canal. Birds that had been singing from the trees in the golden sunset now muted in slumber. Encased in her warm timber cabin, Josie felt alone in the world.

The mournful cry of an owl trickled through the thin windows. With a sigh, Josie placed her glass on the table, the amber liquid it contained rocking as it settled. Slipping her feet into the waiting boots, she eased to her feet and shuffled outside. She had to make a final check on her moorings and fasten the shutters before she would truly be secure.

Pushing open the timber doors, Josie shivered as she stepped into the October evening. Her fingertips tingled as she pulled her hat further over her ears. Staring along the towpath, she gaped at the thick mist swirling over the surface, the cloud of her breath carrying over to join the dance.

In the distance, she could just hear the growl of city traffic, as though the fog had muted the vivacity of life. Tiny lights twinkled close by, following the dark shadow of the canal. The only sign of the reassuring bulk of neighbouring narrow boats swallowed by the night. High above the city, clear of the mist and tree canopy, gleaming lights illuminated the clean stonework of Nottingham Castle, a silent witness to the isolation that she felt around her.

As fog blurred the edge of the canal, Josie had to summon every ounce of nerve to step off the boat. With her heart racing an unseen fear, she hurried to drop the shutters into place, slipping each latch into its slot. Each thump and click disturbing the heavy silence, feeding an anger Josie could sense within the mist. She bit back a squeal as she tripped over the mooring line. Planters rocked in their cradles as she lurched against the boat.

Reaching the bow, Josie stepped back onto the boat, hesitating as she prepared to reach the final shutters away from the reassurance of the path. A muffled tread paced through the mist behind her. Josie froze. Warm breath dusted across the back of her neck.

Closing her eyes, she forced herself to breathe. Something pawed the gravel across the path. Her pulse raced, the blood roaring past her ears. Taking a deep breath, she opened her eyes and turned. Her cry died in her throat as she stared at the solid mass of a riderless black pony. It snorted, tossing his head so a long mane danced on its powerful neck.

Pricking its ears, the stallion paused to stare past Josie into the darkness. A chill of apprehension quivered down her spine.

Glancing over her shoulder towards the dark canal, a white shape fluttered at the edge of her peripheral vision. Tearing her gaze away, she stared at the gleaming moon. Counting, she focused on steadying her breathing. She looked back at the towpath. The stallion blocked her return to the cabin. Metal shoes grated on the dirt as it pawed the ground, ears flat to its head.

"Stay with me ... Play with me..." A plaintive cry floated on the cool air. "Josie..."

Against her will, Josie turned back. Through eyes glazed with tears, she watched transfixed as a girl glided through the darkness. Her white dress clung to her frail body, the fabric heavy with water. Blonde hair draped with weeds framed a pale face. Grey eyes appeared much as Josie remembered, wide and pleading.

A tear broke free of her eyelashes, cutting a cool trail over her cheek. Shaking her head, Josie backed away. Even as her heart clenched, she stumbled back onto the towpath, knowing the stallion was no threat to her, just another ploy to tug at her heart.

"Josie... don't leave..."

Fighting the desperate urge to fling herself into the ghost's welcoming arms, Josie turned and hurried back through the mist to the cabin door. Inside the warm timber hulk she knew she would be safe. Keeping her eyes firmly on the ground, she leapt onto the static boat, flinging the doors open with a crash. The spectre appeared by her side.

"I'm lonely..." the gentle words seeped into Josie's mind, settling down to torment her for another year.

Turning, she offered one last glance. Vision blurred by tears, she didn't need to see to know the details of the pleading face before her.

Swallowing her sobbed reply, she slipped back into the creaking hull, thumping the doors closed as she sank onto the steps. Closing her eyes, she leaned against the thin barrier shaking. She allowed the flood of tears to cool her cheeks unabated.

Five years after the accident she still couldn't find it in herself to leave. She found her mind drifting as it always did to that fateful autumn afternoon.

Her parents had stepped into Nottingham for some last minute shopping leaving her in charge of a sister ten years her junior. Trying desperately to focus on course work, she had grown increasingly irritated by her sister's demands for attention.

*"I want to ride my horse on the towpath."* The lyrical voice still pleaded in Josie's ear.

*"Oh just get out!"* Josie's heart wrenched, hearing her own snapped response once more. They both knew that Marie was never allowed on the towpath unsupervised.

The scream had pierced the cabin.

Josie still felt the chill that had driven her from the narrow boat at a run.

*Bursting through the doors, her gaze fell on the ripples spreading across the smooth surface of the canal. Without hesitating, she dived. She sliced through the dark, icy water without hesitation.*

*Pulling herself towards the epicentre of the ripples, Josie fought against a rising tide of fear. Through the murk, Marie's pale face appeared, eyes wide. Pleading for help. Thick strands of weeds stretched past her, wrapping themselves round her flailing legs and following the lines of her arms as she reached towards Josie. Ignoring the strain in her lungs, Josie surged forward. But as she watched, the light in Marie's eyes faded. Her sister's body sagged into the embrace of water and weeds.*

Opening her eyes to the firelight that warmed the cabin Josie pushed away images of her sisters limp body. Reaching for the glass, she downed the contents, waiting for that reassuring burn as the whiskey cursed through her system.

She had pulled Marie to the surface, into the strong grip of neighbouring boatmen. Moments later, her parents had returned to find her clutching Marie's limp form. They hadn't forgiven her, leaving soon afterwards: driven away by the agonising memories of their youngest daughter. Unable to forgive herself, Josie gave herself to the narrow boat. Committing herself to the eternal pain of remembering.

She knew one day she would give in. One day she would join Marie in the darkness.

# Into the Deep

THE ENDLESS BLUE STRETCHED OUT for miles. Sunlight glistened gold on the surface, ripples of dark and light as the tides danced to the rhythm of the moon. Looking through the clear gem like turquoise, she could see the rocks, pebbles and sand that lined the sea bed below the boardwalk. Fishes darted across, seeking food in the crevices, their shadows rolled across the undulating surface. She longed to feel the liquid wrap her in a cool embrace.

Her hands clutched the metal railings so tight they paled white in the heat of the evening air. She felt a sense of 'future' in the blue horison. Above her, the harsh cries of circling gulls sang crisp and clear. She thought she heard them call her name. Madness. Wisps of hair twirled at her shoulders in a breeze that carried the salty tang of the sea.

Closing her eyes tightly, she shook her head. There is nothing beneath the waves, but death. Her father had proved that. Her therapist, her family, all continued to stress that. So why could she not resist the pull of the water? Why was she drawn to the coast with the same force as the tide?

"There you are Paradita!"

She stiffened as James slid his arm round her waist. His rich voice rung round her head and through her ears. As usual, his presence sent a wave of heat rushing through her body, rippling through every nerve and muscle to settle in her core. But the simmering fire was slowly cooling.

"What are you doing here? I thought we were meeting in the restaurant?"

"I don't know." Shrugging, Paradita turned without releasing her grip on the railings. "I just…"

"Not again Paradita." James scowled down at her. "I thought you'd got over this…again."

"So did I. I want to, I don't understand why… I just…" she turned back to stare across the open expanse of ocean to the grey of the horizon line.

A large cruise ship slipped across the surface, slicing effortlessly through the waves as it headed out for adventure.

"It's just so open… so many possibilities… the future lying open and free."

"Your future is here Paradita. Everything you want, everything you need is with me. On this island." Prising her fingers from the metal, James forced her to turn back to him.

She stared up at him, at his eyebrows that dipped together over brown eyes that gazed at her without a trace of the mischief or compassion that had attracted her. They burned with seriousness and ambition. But with each stern gaze he turned her way, she felt him driving a hammer into her. Not so much curing her of her flights of fantasy, or purging her of the water that sometimes seemed to overwhelm her, just pressurising them until there were times they were all she could focus on, and all she could do to contain them. With this dawning realisation, she knew he would never understand. Could never understand.

With a sigh, she closed her eyes, a wry smile playing at the corner of her lips. She felt the pressure ease with her own understanding. Thinking she was finally agreeing with him, James caressed her jawline with his forefinger, his own thin lips relaxing into a smile.

"Come on, let's go for dinner. I don't know why, but all this fresh air makes me hungry."

With a last lingering look behind her, Paradita followed as he led the way across the road, drawing her away from the water. He grinned down at her, a challenging light in his eyes that she ignored. The soft material of her skirt skimmed her knees as she walked, sparking an inexplicable annoyance at its inconsistent touch.

"Did I tell you how beautiful you look today?" James asked.

She shook her head, her brown ponytail brushing across her bare shoulders as she hoped to preserve the comforting silence.

"Well you do. That vest top does wonders to..." Paradita didn't need to look to know where James was staring.

She was fully aware that the low cut top crossing the rise of her breasts revealed too much. If she weren't so damn hot all the time, she wouldn't wear it. Sometimes it entertained her to note James's disapproval of the admiring looks she attracted from others, a hypocritical side to him that recognised as dangerous.

As it was, she was still too hot and she had barely anything on. The only reason that she had resisted her bikini was the knowledge that James was taking her to his favourite, most expensive, restaurant. Instead of the expected cocktail dress, she had found a delightful bejewelled vest top that perfectly matched her simple white skirt. It was a light alternative to the dress code that would be overlooked because of James's wealth and frequency to the restaurant.

The waiter paused only a moment to take in her outfit and James's embrace before he approached them with a smile. He showed them to a table in the far corner of the restaurant, promising them privacy, whilst keeping her out of sight of the other clientele. Hidden behind the giant fish tank.

"Do you have any idea how lucky I feel?" James declared, staring across the table at her. Keeping a firm grip on her hand, he smoothed his thumb over the skin around her dazzling ring. "That you agreed to marry me and unite our families."

Smiling, Paradita focused on the clear blue water of the tank behind him. Life was vibrant there, full of darting bolts of colour and swaying fronds of seaweed that reached to the bubbles rolling across the surface from the filter. It helped to distract her from the growing disquiet that had been settling in her mind since her acceptance of his proposal. An acceptance that had much to do with her mothers own encouragement, and pleading for family pride.

"You will be so beautiful at the wedding! It will be the biggest and best wedding of the year." James enthused, automatically selecting the wine and dismissing the waiter.

Paradita tore her gaze from the swimming fish, quelling a surge of jealousy at their simple existence. She tried to focus on the menu, seeking out the light seaweed dishes that she longed to taste.

"It will take some planning of course, but I know your mother is up to the task, and has probably already started." James chuckled to himself. "Yes, there will be much to discuss...but I can't wait for you to be my wife. To be able to show you off properly. To give you everything you've ever wanted."

Shivering, Paradita suppressed the urge to ask him what he thought she wanted. She imagined that he shared her mother's expectation of a woman who loved clothes, handbags, shoes, parties and exotic holidays. Instead, she longed for a quiet life, a retreat from society that she had been brought up to participate in. A society who looked at her strangely and wondered.

A slight cough indicated the quiet approach of the waiter. James overruled her request for a small plate of seaweed and shellfish risotto, and ordered a shared seafood platter. Returning the menu with a sigh, she thought she noted a sympathetic grimace from the waiter over James's shoulder. Shaking her away the imaginings, she turned back to the darting gold, silver, red and green treasures of the tank.

"I'll make you the wealthiest, happiest woman on the island." James continued as though they hadn't been interrupted. "We can repair your family home so that once again it will be the cream of the island. Your father's achievements will be recognised and we can move back to the mountains, away from your ridiculous ideas about the ocean."

Paradita shivered at the thought of the distance from the sea, and the confining darkness of the forest. Her mother insisted that it was the best thing for her. Paradita sighed. Maybe it *was*. There was colour and life in the jungle. The flowers bloomed with rich reds and pinks, purple and yellow fruit thrived all year round in the warmth and the moisture trapped by the mountains. But the prevailing colour was green. Not blue. The warmth she remembered from childhood was stifling. The open ocean, the sea breezes and the gleaming blue offered the coolness she craved.

"You will have horses to ride, dogs to train. All the beautiful jewels and clothes you could ask for…We shall have plenty of children in a few years and drive all your demons from your past away. These teenage fantasies of yours, of your father's, will fade. I promise you."

'If not, you will bury them.' Paradita thought to herself.

"But we will get rid of the swimming pool." He scowled. "That memory of your father will be buried with the past."

Paradita turned away, feeling an anger burning her cheeks the way it so often did at the dismissal of her father's death. Although it had happened when she was very young, she could still see the shape of his body drifting in the clear still waters of the recently completed swimming pool. The scandalous suicide was immediately hushed up by the family, but whispers crept round the small island none the less.

Yet, she instinctively knew that her father had been searching for something. He had died trying to reclaim something that had once been his very core. Her heart saddened for him, as she knew that he had lost whatever it was he was striving to find. But she sometimes wondered if perhaps his death was the best resolution to an unachievable quest.

Their meal arrived. James waited for the waiter to leave them in peace before he returned to his sales pitch, enthusing about the proposed honeymoon in Africa that made Paradita feel like she had swallowed a lead weight with the spiced shrimp. Closing her eyes, she took a deep breath. She let his words wash over her, a constant tide that she shut out of her mind as she focused on picking at the plates before them. Whenever he paused, she smiled, nodding and agreeing as she knew he expected.

But however hard she tried, some words found their way in, worming their way into her heart and down to her stomach, leaving a trail of disgust that soon quelled her appetite. Setting down her cutlery, she sipped at the wine, hating the acidic taste as it flowed over her taste buds.

"Will you excuse me if I go to the rest room James?" She asked, putting down the glass.

"Certainly." James paused to sip at his own glass, frowning as he noted her plate. "Are you not well? You've not eaten much?"

"I'm fine. A little hot. I'm just not hungry. That's all."

James shrugged as he turned back to his own lobster claw.

Standing in front of the mirror, she splashed cold water on her face. Her skin tingled with the caress of the droplets. The liquid tantalising and settling tense nerves. Letting rivulets trickle down her cheeks, she stared at her reflection, noting a green glitter in her blue eyes. As the water dried, the sparkle faded and her discontent settled once more into the corner of her mouth, as though the water had momentarily washed away her unhappiness. Convinced she was imagining things, she quickly reapplied her red lip gloss and returned to the table. She paused to study the gleaming scales in the fish tank at close quarters.

"There you are. I was beginning to wonder if you'd escaped." James chuckled, stepping up to her with a stern gaze that didn't match his chuckle.

Paradita noted that the table had been cleared, and a steaming cup of coffee rested on her placemat. She smiled and returned to her chair under the direction of his strong hand in the small of her back. Without comment, she allowed him to push the chair under her as she sat.

"Have I told you how graceful your movements are? The way you glide through the room, slicing your way through the air... sashaying like... it's intoxicating."

Paradita smiled, reaching for her coffee cup. She sensed James give her a funny look as he returned to his own chair and knew he was watching her closely. The silence was not the comforting one that she needed. She winced as the bitter liquid scalded her tongue, and she pushed the mug away. James continued to assess her in silence, holding her gaze, and forcing her to ignore the movements she could see in her peripheral vision.

"Now, will we go back to my flat for some port, or shall we take a stroll to clear away that stomach bug of yours?" James asked, finally placing his own cup back to the table, and calling the waiter over.

"Can we take a walk, the fresh air will…"

"I should point out, sir…" The waiter interjected as he held James's jacket for him "that a wind has got up and Miss didn't bring a coat."

"Right." James nodded. "We'll take a taxi back to the flat."

"I shall call one for you sir." The waiter dipped his head and scurried across the room, weaving through tables as he raced them to the door.

Paradita scowled as James tucked her arm under his and led her to the entrance lobby. His grip tightened as he stopped within the glass case. Palm trees swayed along the beach. Paradita could feel the sweat trickling between her shoulder blades, generated by the sun glaring down at them through the glass. Pulling her arm free, she strode out of the door and across the road to the railings.

As her skirt whipped about her thighs, the wind carried sprays of water from the ocean beneath to her skin. Each kiss of water cooled and refreshed, sending frissons of excitement along her nerves. Instinctively, she untied her hair. It whipped around her head, pulling at her scalp and batting at her face. A bubble of laughter welled in her throat as a sudden exhilaration wound through her.

Beneath her, the depths of the oceans stirred. Streaks of white skimmed the turbulent surface, revealing then hiding glimpses of the serene darkness below. As she watched, dark shapes of mammals and fish eased through the water, swarming and circling beneath her. A sudden burst of agonising jealously flared in her stomach. It spread a fire through her system to her heart. She couldn't just stand and watch any more.

Without hesitation, she clambered onto the handrail. James's angry cry from behind only served to drive her forward faster. She pulled the sequined top over her head, watching as the wind tore it from her grasp and flung it over the dancing waters. Keeping her arms over her head, she leaned forward and pushed away from the handrail.

A cool welcome exploded through her as she sliced through the water. Liquid silk wrapped round her, supporting her as momentum carried her deep into its embrace.

She felt her legs meld, the skin rippling, as they united into one powerful limb. Her feet stretched, the toes forming a long throbbing tail that teased the water.

Turning, she watched transfixed as gleaming green blue scales spread across her skin.

As her hair floated, carried by the current, the skin by her ears tingled and she felt gills drawing oxygen from the water into her lungs. Reaching to the skirt waistband, she noted the webbing that now stretched between her fingers. Flipping the button through its hole, she watched as the material slipped over her tail, drifting to the surface where a crowd had gathered, peering at her from the handrails above.

She spotted James scowling into the water. With a bemused smile, she watched his expression change from anger and shock, to horror as he saw who she truly was. Shaking his head, he backed away, pushing the crowd aside as he tried to distance himself from the creature that had been his fiancée.

Twisting, she looked out into the welcoming darkness of the blue ocean. Her future lay within its depths. With one flick of her tail, she propelled herself forward, reaching out her hands to grasp it.

# Resolution

Edith didn't need to be able to see to know it was raining outside. She could hear the steady dripping of water as it seeped through the roof, starting its descent through her home. The walls were perpetually wet. Peeling wallpaper flapped in the many draughts that rushed through the building. Edith sighed. Pulling the woollen scarf closer about her shoulders, she hunched in her aged armchair. Listening to the fire's crackle in the hearth, she breathed deeply, enjoying the heady odour of the burning wood.

The thud of a key turning in the lock sent Edith further down into her chair. Door hinges creaked.

"Mum?" Edith could hear distaste in Zoe's nasal tones.

"Here." Reluctantly she answered, her voice croaking through lack of use.

"Really mum, you can't stay here like this." Zoe wrinkled her nose as she entered the sitting room. She scowled at the tattered state of her mother's once pink shawl, the dishevelled tangle of hair projecting from beneath her head scarf.

"Why not? This is my home."

"Because mum, it's not ... right."

Making her way further into the room, Zoe perched on the edge of the sofa, careful to minimise her contact with the rotting fabric. She studied Edith carefully. Her face was pale to the point of translucency; the skin wrinkled round dark eyes that gleamed in sharp contrast. Long fingers clutching the shawl close to her chin ended in uneven fingernails lined with dirt.

"Dad wouldn't like to see you like this mum." Zoe hoped to ease the old woman's resolve. "It's time to move..."

"Tcha!" Edith snorted, her thin lips tilting into an unkind sneer. "Your father wouldn't care a jot."

"Then why stay? Why keep yourself in this miserable place?"

Shivering, Zoe glanced round at the room someone had tried to furnish and make a home. The old family portraits had been replaced with modern prints, abstract shapes that clashed with the floral wallpaper. A bold ceramic vase stood in the windowsill, sunflowers and roses trying to bring sweetness and light into the dreary space.

But there was so much work to do. The roof needed repairing and the damp proof course refreshing as a starting point. Only then could the aged decor and the rotting carpets be replaced. Zoe had removed the quality, timber furniture, keeping what she wanted and selling the rest on, but her mothers living room suite, couldn't be moved. They had tried. She shivered. With the damp and the broken heating, the room was perpetually cold. Even without her mother's presence.

"I'm waiting."
"For what?"
"Him."
"Who...? Oh mum, you don't think dad's coming back do you?"
"That pile of shit? Why in hell would I wait for him to return?! He's never coming back."

There was a gleam of certainty from her mother's blind eyes that made Zoe shiver. It had been years since her father's last visit, when he descended on the family, grovelling for forgiveness and promising never to leave again. Yet his visit was even briefer than usual. He vanished without a word. As her mother had grown colder and more isolated with his every return, Zoe had forgiven his absences, desperate perhaps for a loving figure, or sympathetic to his near crazy love-hate fixation with her mother.

Zoe had frequently pleaded with him to take her away, but each time he had refused. Life on the road was no place for a young child he said. After his final visit, her mother had relaxed, started to smile more, but never at Zoe. Nothing changed in the way that Zoe had been treated.

Edith continued to stare unseeing into the red heart of the fireplace. She loathed her daughter's visits as much as she had despised her husband's. She had finally taken the courage to do something about him, but she knew she couldn't do anything about Zoe. Her fading strength ensured that she remained a pitiful, lonely creature.

"So, who are you waiting for?" Zoe's voice droned through the quiet space, slicing through Edith's patience with the dexterity of a carving knife.

"Never you mind." She snarled. "He is coming, I know he is. And then, and only then, will I leave! This is my home!" The fire guard quivered. "Now, leave me in peace!"

A cold draught blasted through the room. Several of the pictures rocked on their hooks.

"Please mum, just think about it?" Zoe asked, standing. "I hate to see you like this."

"Then stop coming round!"

"It's not for me. You have to let the people..."

"They invade my house and expect me to accept it!" Edith shrieked.

A glass clock crashed to the floor, inches from Zoe's delicately clad feet.

With one last look at her wild mother, Zoe strode from the room, firmly closing the door behind her. There was no doubting that she needed to work out a way of moving her. The house needed clearing, needed cleansing. She needed help, but didn't know who to turn to. Her husband didn't believe her but refused to accompany her to visit the rotting ruin, claiming the mould did nothing for his asthma. But she had seen his nerves on the one visit he had made, the pallor in his skin, his eagerness to leave the unnaturally cold room.

---

"She's getting worse!" She shouted as she closed the door to her own home half an hour later.

"Sure she is honey." Mark sniffed sticking his head out from the kitchen.

"Oh I know you don't believe me, but surely you can see that the place is becoming uninhabitable." She flicked off her shoes, tucking them carefully onto their allotted space in the shelf.

"Nothing a good builder can't sort. Tea?"

"Oo, yes please." Zoe padded through to the kitchen and settled onto the barstool. "They are good builders… but they can't get anywhere near without things flying at them…The clock has come off the wall again."

"Breeze in a draughty house or a dodgy hook… or both." Mark grunted. "There are some interesting personal ads in the paper today by the way."

"What?"

"Have a look in the personal ads section."

The water splashed in her favourite mug as Mark poured from the kettle. She watched him intently, although after five years of marriage he knew well enough not to leave the tea bag in the water as he went for the milk.

"Why would I do that? I've got to figure out what to do with mum?"

"Just read it." Mark sighed, placed the mug next to the folded paper.

Puzzled, Zoe watched him return to the counter where he was preparing the vegetables for their evening meal. As though sensing her gaze, he glanced over his shoulder, raising an eyebrow at her.

"Fine." Zoe sniffed.

Closing her fingers round the smooth paper, she unfolded it and spread it across the breakfast bar.

"We are not getting a dog Mark." Zoe glared up at him as she noted the Labrador puppies for sale.

"I know." Mark shrugged. "I was just looking. That wasn't what I want you to see."

"Can't you just tell me?"

"Not as well as the ad will. Keep reading."

Growling in frustration, she sipped at her tea and continued to read through a pointless jumble of words selling furniture, or finding toys. But half way through a name caught her attention, and she returned to the start of the ad.

*Jenny Stanford of Stapleford, would like to contact Dominic Mortense. Please contact the editor to arrange a meeting.*

Zoe stared. She read the ad again.

"See." Mark grinned at her. "I told you there were some interesting ads in the paper today."

"Why does she want to see father?" Zoe glanced up, puzzled. "Who is she?"

"I don't know, do I? I take it you don't know a Jenny Stanford."

"No... I don't think so..."

"Well, you'll just have to get in touch, won't you? Stapleford isn't that far, just over the hill... She could have ..."

"But she doesn't want me, she wants..."

"Zoe. You haven't seen your father in twenty years. Is it likely that he will see this ad? No. So someone needs to tell her this."

"Mmm, I suppose…"

"And while you are there, you can find out what her connection is to your father. Who knows, she may have information that you need."

---

Clutching the paper in her hand, Zoe knocked three times on the red door. She frowned as she realised her pulse was racing. Something was telling her that this was important, but she couldn't see what this council estate house had to offer her. A small white haired woman opened the door. Seeing the paper in her hand, the woman smiled.

"Zoe Wallace?"

"Yes, that's me." Zoe smiled.

"Do come in dear."

Zoe stepped into a hallway filled with golden light from the open door, and followed the woman into a large sitting room.

As she settled into the floral sofa Zoe looked round, automatically noting the furniture and ornaments crammed into the room. Two ceramic spaniels sat either side of the electric fire, beneath a sweeping wooden mantelpiece capped with a plethora of Royal Crown Derby birds. The wallpaper was hidden behind paintings of agricultural or coastal scenes.

"You are Dominic and Edith Mortense's daughter you said?" The old woman sat cautiously opposite Zoe.

"Yes, that's right." Zoe frowned. "You wanted to contact my father …"

"I do. Have you been able to contact him?"

"I haven't seen him for years." Zoe shook her head. "That's what I'm here for really. I have no way of knowing if he will ever see your ad, so I thought it only fair to tell you…"

"I understand." Jenny nodded. "But, you've come in person because…?"

"Because I want to know what your connection is. My mother is of the firm opinion that he won't be coming back at all and …"

"Your mother? I thought that she…" Jenny Stanford paled. "I thought she died…"

"She is,…did… I'm…I'm sensitive, and she has been causing problems.…"

"Oh."

"She says she is waiting for someone… a man … not my father…" Zoe stopped, frowning to herself and turning away from the woman's sympathetic gaze. She didn't need to tell this complete stranger the problems she was facing.

"I see." Jenny Stanford paused. "Would you like a cup of tea?"

"No thank you, I don't want…"

"You should dear…It's no trouble." Baffled, Zoe watched her disappear.

---

"Here we go my love." Jenny reappeared, pushing a tea trolley carefully arranged with china teacups, a teapot and tissues.

"This is all very nice, Mrs Stanford…"

"Jenny my dear."

"Jenny, but I don't see…"

"I'm afraid this is not an easy tale to tell." Jenny poured the tea, oblivious to Zoe's protests.

"Tale?" Zoe watched the stream of golden brown liquid with distaste.

"Yes dear. I wanted to discuss this with your father… but if he isn't around…" Jenny sat back in her chair, sipping her tea, eyes glazed.

"What did you want to discuss with my father?" Zoe prompted after a moment.

Jenny jolted, looking up at Zoe with an apologetic smile.

"Sorry dear. The challenge of getting old, a wandering mind." Jenny's cup rattled on the saucer as she settled it on the table by her side.

"Your father and my husband, Jim, grew up together. They were at school and they went on into the building trade together. We were at each others weddings all those years ago." She paused to look across at the sepia photograph resting at the edge of a bookcase crammed with titles.

"Your father got out, and went into sales while my Jim worked on site for forty years. All local jobs and the like. When your father started to travel, we drifted out of contact. At least, I thought that was why your mother and I…"

"You see, it turns out that my dear Jim …" A gleam of tears spread across her eyes.

"My dear Jim had been… My Jim was …" She took a deep breath. "Jim was having an affair with your mother." A droplet escaped the mass and trickled down her cheek. "It had been going on for years ..."

Zoe gaped. Her mother having an affair was not something she could process. Not the cold, distant woman she knew.

"I only found out last week, when ..." Jenny sobbed, pausing to reach for a tissue. "My poor Jim was knocked down, and it's upset his mind. He was calling for your mother and raved something about your father that frightens me. I hoped that he...well, that you could ...dispel my fears."

"Fears...?" Zoe whispered.

"Something Jim said... I could barely make it out, but ..." Jenny paused, tears streaming unchecked. "It sounded like ... like Jim and your mother ... like they had consorted to ...to...get rid of him."

Zoe gaped.

"I thought I was imagining it .. I hope I was ... His actual words sounded like...*after we did...now he's out the way, we just...*" Sniffing, Jenny drew a handkerchief from her pocket, pausing to wipe her cheeks.

"I got some dates out of him and I... I remember him being somehow absent...long days on site... they were building a new school, I didn't think anything of it. He came home one evening all wired up, ... jumpy and tense all week... I can remember wondering how he didn't do himself an injury." Jenny shook her head.

"Then he was as depressed as I ever saw him the following weekend. Said it was down to the football or whatever...I didn't believe him, but I never thought...

Oh my Jim!" Jenny dropped her head into her hands sobbing.

Zoe stared. Her head buzzed. Jenny's cracking voice continued, but was drowned out by Zoe's memories of her mother's long-standing contempt of her father. Her certainty of his never returning. Zoe's pulse raced. Her father's round smiling face, long forgotten suddenly resurfaced. With it, a sweeping guilt for his unquestioned absence.

"When did you last see your father dear?" Jenny asked quietly some moments later, watching the unsteady rise and fall of Zoe's blouse. "I hope I'm wrong…"

"I… um…I was twelve…so, um…twenty years ago." She looked at Jenny hopefully. "It was the spring, I can remember the daffodils being out, but not being happy about it. Can't stand them now."

"Twenty years… so that would be…Oh my dear…" Jenny gaped. "That would be when… early March I think they were working on foundations…"

Zoe stared.

"No, that can't be right." Scowling she shook her head. "You think that my mother, and your husband… you think they killed my father. Ridiculous." Pushing herself to her feet glowered down at the old woman. "This isn't a TV show. It's real life, and if you think I'm going to listen to this babble…"

Turning, she stormed across the room to the door. As she did so, a collection of photographs spread across the telephone table caught her gaze. They were black and white images of two couples sharing a picnic. Pausing, she reached out her hand to the top collection, her fingers skimming the hard edges as they began to curl.

A man and a woman sat towards the front of the blanket, smiling happily into the camera. By the side of a woman, a man sat slightly back of them, glancing across at the woman who sat at the other side of the blanket. There was no disguising the passion in their stare. Zoe's heart clenched. The man staring into the camera was her father. The woman by his side, staring at the other man, was her mother.

Picking up the other photographs, she flicked through them. Images of her mother and father showed a besotted man, but a coldly indifferent woman,. A woman whose smiles where enforced to play the required part of a happy marriage. Zoe froze as she found the last picture. A young child was clutched in her father's arms as he smiled down at her. Behind him her mother glared at the back of his head with an intensity that sent shivers down Zoe's spine.

"I'm sorry dear."

Zoe jumped as Jenny placed a withered hand on Zoe's arm. "I found those in the attic. When Jim started saying… I wanted to remember, wanted to prove he was … I don't know. Wrong I suppose." Jenny shook her head, teasing the first photograph from Zoe's grip. "But I didn't… I think I proved it. Look how besotted they are."

"You can't think…" Zoe whispered, a churning weight of certainty settling in her stomach.

"I'm afraid I do." Jenny nodded her head sadly. "I think my husband, my poor foolish, stupid, heartless Jim, and your mother killed your father. I'm not sure we will ever be able to prove it, not without destroying that school, but I think they did."

"Then why aren't they...?"

"I don't know." Jenny shrugged, a tear glinting on her cheek. "Perhaps because of me... I was pregnant with my son then, Jim promised never to abandon us... then your mother died and..." Jenny shook her head, straightening and smiling gently at Zoe.

"I'm really so sorry to have to tell you this, my dear. I can't begin to imagine how you must be feeling, how you must hate..."

Zoe stared blindly at the wall. She didn't know what she felt. Her heart was racing. She felt cold. The tears she should have felt at her mother's betrayal, and father's demise only stuck in her throat. Her mother had never loved her father; Zoe had recognised that even as a child. She realised she didn't hate her mother; she didn't feel anything for her.

"I'm alright, really." Shaking herself she took a deep breath and smiled across to Jenny. "How is your husband?"

"Jim's... not good." Jenny shook her head sadly. "He's barely conscious, and very weak. He's lasted longer than expected."

"I'm sorry."

"Don't you worry about it dear. He's an old man. Come back and have some tea dear, it will help with the shock."

Obediently, turned, following Jenny back into the living room. Her mind was whirling as she sank back onto the sofa and reached for her teacup. She grimaced as the tepid bitter liquid slipped over her tongue. Frowning, she tried to sort out the revelations. A life time of deception with a murderous conclusion. An explanation for her father's final abandonment. But the story was unfinished.

The two lead characters were somehow adrift. Jim suffered in hospital while her mother lingered in a family home no longer hers to occupy. An innocent family subjected to the hauntings of a woman long since isolated from her family and an innocent wife shaken to her core.

"Could he...Is he waiting for something do you suppose?" She mused.

"Pardon dear?"

"Does he seem to want my mother?"

"I don't know... he might... I suppose." Jenny frowned. "But I don't see..."

"We can help each other perhaps. My mother is refusing to leave. She is preventing the new owners of her home from developing it... and it needs it desperately..."

"She's a..."

"Yes." Zoe nodded. "She's haunting my family home.... If your husband is not well...I know it must hurt you to face the prospect that he ..."

"It's his suffering I can't stand." Jenny declared. "And if he did..., even if it was only intended..., then he doesn't deserve... I'm better off rid of him. Start afresh. Even at my age that is possible." She blushed.

Zoe studied Jenny carefully, smiling at the strength in her blue eyes.

"Then I suggest your father pays a visit to my mother."

Two days later, Zoe let them into the house.

"What do you want now?!" Edith's voice cut through the dank stillness.

"I've brought someone to meet you."

Zoe pushed Jim's wheelchair silently across the room to the worn armchair. Trembling by her side, Jenny clutched the drip stand, saline bag swinging. Jimmy hunched under the protective cover layers of tightly wrapped blankets. His breath rasped in his chest, as he fought to cling to a life slowly ebbing from his once strong frame.

"Who is..."

"Edith?" Jim croaked.

Zoe watched aghast as her mother's face lit up.

"Jimmy? You've come for me at last!" She reached out.

"You've been waiting...?"

"I promised I would Jim."

"So you did." The old man nodded. His eyes closed, his hand gripping the ghost hand of his love.

Zoe's heart thumped in her chest. Tears inexplicably filled her eyes. She felt a gentle touch at her fingers. Closing her fingers round Jenny's quivering hand, she glanced over and noted tears glinting on the woman's cheeks. Jenny looked across at her with a watery smile. Turned back they watched the last breath hiss through Jim's lips. As he sagged into death, silence descended. Zoe watched Edith fading away, a grin of delight etched on her face.

# Revelations

"How can you be so excited?!" Sophie muttered, glancing across at Roxie as they stood at the edge of the car park, leaning against the metal fence that prevented them stepping too close to the cliff.

Roxie was practically quivering with anticipation, staring out across the abandoned quarry. Golden sunlight glittering on the turquoise lake below reflected as dancing jewels on the dark slate walls. High above, a pair of broad winged buzzards glided across the pale blue sky.

Dyed green hair whipped at Roxie's shoulders, skimming across cheeks stretched tight into a grin. Her green eyes focused on the space stretching before them, following the almost invisible wire across the clear sky.

"It looks terrifying!"

"Do you not want to do this?" Roxie turned, a concerned look immediately falling across her face. She noted the pallor in Sophie's cheeks as she fidgeted with tying and retying her blonde hair.

"We booked as I understood everyone on the team was up for this. I don't want anyone to do something if they don't want ..."

"No, no, it's fine… I'm up for giving this a go…" Sophie smiled. "It's just that … it's bigger than I thought it would be…"

"Yes, it is big." Roxie turned back with a grin.

"Be over with quickly though." Mike sniffed from behind. "Fastest wire in the world this one."

"Really?" Sophie's eyebrows twitched.

"Oh yes." Simon nodded. "Fastest and longest. We'll definitely get our moneys worth."

"Trust the accountant to think of that." Mike scoffed.

"Someone has to."

"Now now boys." Roxie turned her back on the beckoning void of the quarry, smiling at the rest of the team. "Are we ready?"

"Yes!"

"I guess…"

"Erm…"

"Anyone who doesn't want to do this doesn't have to." Roxie noted. "There is still time to change your mind. As Sophie has observed, it is rather big…"

"But we've paid for fifteen tickets…" Simon hissed.

"Then I shall use up the remaining goes." Roxie's teeth gleamed. "I know the owners and I'm sure they won't mind."

"You know…"

"So, you're the Dragon design team?" A deep voice boomed across from the timber clad building to their right. "Are we ready to fly?"

Roxie turned, smiling at the broad shouldered figure beaming down at them. Drake was dressed in the scarlet jumpsuit and black harness that identified him as an instructor. His own red hair clipped close to his head.

"Yes, I think we are." Roxie nodded.

"That's what I like to hear. Come on in and get changed." He stepped aside, and Roxie led the way.

She smiled at Clarissa behind the welcome desk and continued to the changing area, where a mass of black suits hung from poles lining the walls. The fabric rustled as she rummaged for her size.

"You'll need to find a suit that you can slip over your existing clothes." Drake instructed to the rest of the team, casting a shadow across the room as he stood in the doorway. He examined the small group, nodding in approval at the simple sports gear they wore. "You can leave your jumpers here. I presume your valuables are in the bus with the driver?"

"Yes." Roxie nodded, drawing a suit towards her.

The room filled with rustling as the others searched for their suits. Roxie settled on the bench to remove her trainers before slipping her feet into the trouser legs. The material welcomed her, smoothing over her leggings with a gentle caress. She shivered with excitement. It didn't matter how many times she did this, the thrill never paled.

Standing, she teased the suit up her curved frame, easing her arms through the sleeves. The zip whirred as she pulled the fastening into place. She watched the rest of the team settling into their own suits as she flicked the bobble from her wrist, reaching back to tie her hair into submission.

"Looking good doll." Drake murmured.

"Why thank you." She whispered back without turning, wiggling her hips and chuckling as she heard the deep growl in his chest.

"Vixen."

"Alright. What's next?" Mike asked, clapping his hands together as he straightened.

"When we're all ready, we'll find you a helmet and a harness before we get you onto the bus." Drake sniffed. He looked round the room, noting the last few zips were being pulled into place. "All set? Then off we go."

Roxie waited as Mike followed Drake, leading the team out. She fell in line with Sophie and watched her with concern. The blonde girl smiled weakly at her, patting at her hair to ensure all stray wisps were in place before slipping her right finger into her mouth. She scowled, pulling it free and Roxie noted the uneven edge of the nail.

"Please, don't feel pressured into this." She urged.

"I don't." Sophie smiled. "I want to do this, to try something new… I like a good rollercoaster. I just prefer the ones where I'm sat down and strapped in, with other people next to me. Going it alone on this, with only a small harness… I'm nervous." She shrugged. "Besides, if I didn't do this, what do we talk about in the pub afterwards…"

"That isn't the point …"

"Here you go Roxie." Drake shoved a harness into her arms.

She stopped abruptly, startled. He grinned down at her.

"And here's one for you miss. Now, I need everyone to listen carefully..." Drake turned away, falling into serious safety mode.

Roxie zoned him out, automatically following his instruction from long practice as she scanned the team watching him intently. The diversity of her staff always fascinated her, and she always delighted in learning new things and pushing for new skills during these annual bonding sessions.

The group automatically divided into the artists and the administrators. No competition between them that she was aware of, just different personalities that ensured her company thrived.

"And to adjust your hat... Roxie, are you missing something?!" Drake asked, jolting her train of thoughts.

She looked up in time to see the white safety hat flying towards her. Her hands flashed out automatically.

"Catch." Drake dipped his head, impressed. "To adjust your hat, put it on your head, clip the latch shut, like this... then reach back and you will feel a small wheel at the base of your skull. Roll that and you will find the helmet tightens or loosens round your head. Once that is comfortable, you will need to adjust the straps round your chin. Please ensure that this is tight, but you will need to be able to put two fingers between the fabric and your skin."

Drake paused, watching as the group adjusted their kits.

"All set?"

A murmur swept through the group, and they nodded.

"Very good. Lets get going then." He turned, leading the way round in front of the building back to the car park.

As they crunched along the gravel path, the pair of buzzards cried overhead, circling in partnership as they surveyed their kingdom. Roxie paused, turning back to stare across the quarry. A shiver ran down her spine. Scanning the bare rock, she pondered the strange feeling that they were being watched She shook her head, and turned back to follow the group.

Her team were climbing into the big red lorry that served as a shuttle bus, and she lengthened her stride to catch them up. Pulling herself after Sophie, she nodded to Glen sitting behind the wheel. Drake's brother filled the cab, grinning back. Only his nose distinguished him from his twin, broken in one of their innumerable childhood fights.

"Alright Doll?"

As she settled onto the metal bench, pulling the seatbelt across her waist she grinned at the team.

"Well, here we go!"

"Mmm." Pale faces stared back at her, eyes wide with nerves and excitement.

They jolted up the uneven dirt track. The truck engine roared, filling the space and blending with the rattle of stones, and jangle of fastenings. Sunlight filtering through the flapping canvas walls covered them all in a warm glow. Roxie felt a trickle of sweat down her spine, and skim her forehead. Closing her eyes, she leaned back, ignoring the uncomfortable press of the harness between her shoulders. She could smell the dry dust and the sweat of bodies in the confined space mingle with the diesel that fuelled the truck's forward momentum.

As the truck wove its way up the mountain, she heard a few whimpers and mutterings. They all knew how close to the edge of the quarry the track ran, and they were taking blind faith that Glen knew what he was doing. After five years, Roxie knew that he did, but for first time visitors the experience was un-nerving. All part of the company drive to heighten the anticipation.

Jerking the team in their seats, the truck stopped.

"Here we go." Glen stuck his head through from the cabin. "Everybody out."

With a chorus of clicks, the team freed themselves from the constraints of their seatbelts. Standing, Roxie followed them to the back of the truck where Glen stood offering a helping hand as they jumped to the ground.

"That was a hideous... ooo!"

"Wow."

"Oh my!"

Roxie smiled as she listened to the ripples of appreciation sweep through the team. She knew exactly what had so impressed them.

Standing near the top of the mountain, the jump platform provided stunning views over Snowdonia, while the mountain formed a comforting mass of rock behind them. Peaks and valleys dominated the landscape, drawing the gaze from the ground to the sky in one instant. Sunlight gilded the jagged crags and ridges, where glimpses of white hid in shadows as a lingering reminder of the snow cladding that winter provided each year. The greenery of the fields and forests stretched up the mountain sides. Straining to reach the summit, they always fell short, over powered by the mass of grey blue slate that cascaded from the sky.

Before them, the mountain disappeared, dropping into the dark void of the quarry. Roxie left the lorry, the engine purring as it cooled. Standing by the edge, she closed her eyes enjoying the gentle skim of cool air on her cheeks, as she listened to the melodic song of the larks and the gentle murmur of the team behind her.

"So, who's going first?" Glenn asked, his deep voice cutting through her reverie.

She turned, and noted the team had gathered by the start of the zip wire. Aware that she had missed Glen's instruction, she flashed him an apologetic smile. The team exchanged glances, as they stared down the wire. They shifted backwards as they had to face the final step.

"Tell you what. As your boss thinks she's such an expert she can miss my instructions, she can show you how it's done?" Glen suggested. "And who'll miss the boss, really?!"

Roxie chuckled and stepped up to the harness.

"Alright. Unless anyone else…"

The team shook their head, looking anxiously on as she was fastened in. She grinned, waving at them before holding her arms by her side as she was lowered onto her front. As Glen clicked the final connections in place, her gaze followed the zip wire. Staring out into the open sky.

"Ready?" Glen bellowed.

"Ready!"

Air rushed past her as she lurched out into the void. The whirr of the wire and the whoosh of air filled her head. Heart hammering, she flew over the quarry. She laughed. The presence of the mountain disappeared behind her. Over sailing the lake, she followed her own reflection slicing across the water. A black blur against the still blue. She sailed over the speckled chipping mountains and gazed down on the waving foliage of trees that had found a sheltered spot in the embrace of the slate.

Watching the land approach, she fought to control herself. The thrill of the flight was nothing to the sense of power she had from controlling her basic instincts. As the wire climbed, she slowed. The air skimming her cheeks softened. She began to hear more sounds above the thundering air. A bird was singing in the trees as she flew above it. Metal jangled as her harness was caught and she jolted to a halt.

Breathing hard, she laughed up at Drake, who grinned down at her.

"You've done it again." He shook his head and reached for her fastenings. "I don't know how you do it. You're the only one I know who can resist."

"With age comes control." She chuckled. Pulling herself to her feet. "Who's behind me?"

Turning, she watched another body come speeding towards her.

"Wohoo!" Mike yelled as he eased to a stop. "That was awesome!"

"I know, right?!" Roxie waited for Drake to release Mike from his harness before offering him a hand, pulling him upright.

"Such a great idea this."

---

"So, it's just Sophie to come?" Roxie turned as Simon stabilised himself.

"Yeah. She kept putting it off… I wonder if she'll go back with…" He nodded, joining the rest of the team who were still buzzing at the quarry edge.

"Here comes Sophie!" Chloe squealed, pointing. "Come on Soph!"

Roxie turned, watching with the rest of the group as the black dart that was Sophie zipped towards them. Two cracks sliced through the air. Sophie's scream echoed round the quarry.

"Oh my God!"

"Sophie's falling!"

"They were shots!"

Roxie didn't hesitate. Setting off at a run, she headed for the unfenced quarry edge. Focused on Sophie, she barely registered the shouts from behind her. As her foot felt the edge of the metal platform, she launched herself forward.

"Roxie! What the hell…!"

"Oh My God she's going jump!"

Over the hum of blood through her ears she heard the rip of fabric. Her shoulders rippled, her wings snapping the harness as they extended. Muscles strained across her back as she gave a powerful flap, pulling herself through the air.

"What in God's name…!"

"How…!"

"What…!"

"My God!"

"Damn it Roxie!"

"I knew it!" An alien voice bellowed from above.

The tug and stretch of muscles was so familiar she barely noticed. She blinked, searching for Sophie as her face twisted, stretching into its reptilian length and tugged her vision out of momentary focus. Sophie was flailing as she hurtled head first towards the slate. Roxie could see her eyes clenched shut, watched the billow of the jumpsuit surrounding Sophie's slender body.

Stretching out arms stiff with scales, Roxie grabbed for Sophie. Her fingers closed around an arm. Sophie jerked, legs swinging as Roxie climbed. Curving her neck, Roxie checked her hold. Lifting Sophie to her chest, she wrapped her arms round her and held her tight.

*'I've got you Sophie.'* She pulsed the thought to Sophie, trying to cut through the panic whirling through her mind.

Sophie jerked. Her scream died in her chest. The deafening rush of wind eased, replaced by a steady pulse of air. Feeling a firm grip on her arm, she prised her eyes open. She was no longer falling. Instead, the quarry cliffs were falling away beneath her. A blur of movement caught her peripheral vision. Turning her head, she watched a large wing beat by her side. A huge, leathery wing.

Feeling an arm wrap round her, she was pulled towards a large, green chest. Her gaze followed the great scales upwards. She screamed. A lizard-like muzzle with two huge yellow eyes stared at her from the end of a long green neck.

*'I've got you Sophie. I've got you.'* Sophie stared as Roxie's face flickered across the reptile face, her words filling Sophie's head.

'What..?!'

A ripple of explosions filled the quarry. The reptilian neck whipped round. Sophie felt the beast jerk, the chest swelling with a deafening roar.

Roxie dipped her shoulder, swooping down to follow the cliff edge. Pain darted up her hind leg. Gunfire followed her as she swept round the slate. Restrained by the overhead wires, she circled the trees. Eyeing the ground below, she watched the team racing for the cabin. Bullets tore through her wings, biting into her shoulder and lodging deep into her tail. Swerving, she roared.

Keeping Sophie beneath her, she scanned the cliff sides for the source of the gunfire. Glen was clambering over the slates, his red-brown scales rippling in the sunlight.

*'I've got this.'* He thought called. *'Get yourself to ground.'*

Glen slipped onto the plateau behind two men. He watched them for several moments, counting his breathing to hold his anger in check.

"Yes, yes, that's it! We've nearly got her!" One man squirmed against a slate pile, peering over the top with binoculars pressed to his face. The second man was crouching, still and controlled, the barrel of a machine gun that was stabilized on a tripod pressed against his cheek.

Changing back to his human form, Glen strode forward oblivious to the cold wind on his bare skin. Reaching out, he closed his fists around the thick collars of their camouflage jackets. He yanked them backwards. The machine gun flicked to the sky before falling silent. The men flailed at his feet.

Hoisting them off the ground, he turned towards them and snarled. The binocular man whimpered.

"If you were looking for the Welsh dragon, you got the wrong one!"

Slamming their foreheads together, he flung their unconscious bodies to ground. Striding across to the plateau edge, he scrambled up the slate, and stared down across the quarry.

*'Drake, I've got them. Clarissa, is Rhys on his way?'*

*'Yes Glen, he'll be with us shortly.'* Clarissa shared.

*'Good. Glen, stay there and I'll go for Roxie.'* Drake instructed

Glen slipped back down to the two men. He didn't want to watch Roxie, fearing that it might be the last time he could. Crossing to the men's bags, he rummaged and found a couple of cable ties. He cranked them tightly around their wrists, resisting the urge to kick the still figures.

Ignoring the pain burning across her shoulder, Roxie beat her wings, drawing away from the trees. Beyond the lake, a shallow beach offered a landing out of the reach of the automatic rifle. Pain exploded across her back. Her vision blurred. She felt the membrane tear across her other wing. The air pressure shifted beneath her, with nothing to give her lift. Blinking, she desperately tried to regain her focus.

*'I'm sorry Sophie, this is going to be rough!'*

Roxie tucked her wings close as she dived towards the lake. As her nose dipped into the lake, she tilted, slamming the water with her shoulder to protect Sophie. Cold sliced over her. Her tail slapped into the blue. Fighting to ignore the agonized complaints of her muscles, she lifted her head, striking out for the surface.

Seeing the rippling outline of the sun through the shadowy water, she lifted her head and fought towards the surface. Her muscles burned as the bullets and cold tormented every nerve ending. Weaving her body and pushing with her hind legs, she climbed. As her nose crested the waves, she gulped a lungful of fresh air. Pain burst across her shoulder as she tried to release Sophie. Crying out, she sank with a mouthful of icy water. Surging forward again, she prised Sophie from beneath her immobile right shoulder. Holding her arm to her chest, she hoisted Sophie to the surface.

Listening to Sophie coughing, spluttering for air, Roxie strained to keep her above the waves. She felt the tug of the depths, the water trying to pull her heavy body deeper. Roxie peered forward. The dark shadow of the cliff loomed before them, but she had no idea how close it was. They needed to get out of the water. Her mind whirled.

*'Sophie, can you take hold of my neck? I can't hold you and get us out of here...'*

*'I... yes...Like this?'*

Feeling Sophie's arms wrap round her Roxie nodded. Releasing her, she felt Sophie's body thumped into her chest, the harness and jumpsuit pulling Sophie down. Roxie strained forward. Pulling herself through the water with her one foreleg she felt at her weakest. Her hind legs and tail burned; thrust adding extra pain to a spine dotted with agonies. She fought to focus through her whirling mind. Water lapped at her ears, cresting over her nose and splashing against her encased eyes.

Her nose batted into the cliff. Stretching out, she clasped her claws into the stone. She let her body drift against the cliff, locking her hind feet against the slate. Pressed against the comforting mass, she gulped for air. She felt Sophie struggling at her shoulder, twisting away from her neck to cling to the cliff. The weight at her neck eased as Sophie managed to find a handhold.

"There's a cave up there!" Sophie cried, her voice shrill with terror and cold.

Sweeping her head, Roxie strained to see it.

*'It's up to your left.'* Drake's deep voice rippled into her mind. *'You can make it.'*

Reassured, Roxie took a deep breath.

*'Come on Sophie. Hold on ... one last push...'*

Shaking, Sophie reached out for the green neck that stretched past her along the slate. The water had sliced through the jumpsuit, sticking the light fabric to her skin. Glancing over her shoulder as the dragon surged forward, she noted the trails of blood that spread across the churning lake water. She gritted her teeth as the slate jolted her shoulder. Her legs were heavy, locked together and banging against the cliff as Roxie climbed. She had never felt so helpless.

She could see bullet holes amidst Roxie's splintered scales, red lines streaking back over her large body. Her mind whirled. Bullets, falling, dragons, blood. It all felt incredibly unreal. She looked up, seeking the sun and sky. A large red dragon peered down at her. She gaped.

Roxie hesitated as her head dipped into the cave mouth. The air was musty, heavy with the scent of dragon.

*'This is your nest!'*

*'Yes, it is.'* Drake agreed. *'Go in.'*

*'I don't want to imposition...'*

*'Damn it Roxie, just get inside. Now is not the time for formalities.'*

Grunting, Roxie pulled herself into the cave. She felt Sophie drop from her neck. Pausing she glanced round, listening to hear Sophie dragging herself to the side of the cave. Satisfied that Sophie was out of her way, she continued into the darkness, curling into a ball and succumbing to the pain washing through her body.

She didn't move as she heard the scape of claws and scales follow them inside. A burst of flame seared the air behind her.

*'Here you go Sophie.'*

Sophie quivered as the red dragon loomed over her. A crackling fire danced in the centre of the cave, ignited by a blast of flame from his mouth. He reached forward, stretching a claw to her. She scrabbled backwards. Pausing, he dipped his head.

*'Would you like me to remove the harness?'*

"I... er... yes please..."

*'Unless you want a very personal view, I'm afraid I'm going to have to stay in this form.'* The rich voice of Drake the instructor almost chuckled in her mind. *'Dearest Roxie is currently lying on my wardrobe.'*

"I...er... ooh." Sophie stilled, staring over at green dragon, scales glittering in the firelight. Her long head was wrapped out of sight behind the bulk of her hindquarters streaked with blood. "Is she alright?"

The red dragon looked up thoughtfully.

*'I don't know. Roxie's tough, been through a lot, but this is going to take some mending.'* He swung his head back to look at her. *'But looking at her, I don't think it's just the bullets that are hurting.'*

"What do you mean?"

*'That's a dejected dragon. But don't you worry about her; we'll take good care of her. You just come here and get warm.'*

Sophie sagged as she felt the dragon's claw slicing through the harness surrounding her legs. The dragon stepped away, his tail sliding across the dirt floor. He crossed to peer down at Roxie. He studied the flare of bullet marks across her. Sophie fumbled with the rest of the harness, dragging the straps over her shoulder. She pulled herself to her feet and staggered across to the fire. The heat seeped across her skin, slowly eating into the chill of water.

"Why would she be dejected? I know she'll be in I can't bear to think what pain, but..."

*'Why do you need to know? What good will it do if you know that she is a dragon who has just revealed herself to a group of humans she sees as family?'* Drake snorted, turning to glare at her. *'What good will it do now that she has to leave all she loves and move on again? The one happiness she has had in centuries. What good will it do if you know that she has exposed the whole of her race to the Lords know what terrorism?'*

Sophie gaped. Drake strode past her, returning to stand and stare across the lake from the cave mouth.

The purr of an engine floated into the cave. Drake straightened.

*'Here's your ride.'* He turned to look at her.

"Right..." Sophie stepped forward then paused. "Does Roxie not need...I mean..." She glanced over her shoulder.

*'She can't.'* Drake sighed. *'Aside from the fact if she changed back she'd be naked, she needs to heal first. Too much damage and the change can't happen.'* Drake snorted. *'Though why I'm telling you Lords only know.'*

"Oh." Sophie looked back at Roxie, her heart sinking.

She didn't want to leave Roxie. It was clear that she was in a lot of pain, and Sophie wanted to help as Roxie had helped her so often in the past. She looked back at Drake, who was watching her, tail twitching.

"Will she..."

*'She'll be fine. We look after our own.'*

"Of course... right..." Sophie hesitated, hearing a thump of rubber against the rock. "I just..."

"Miss Sophie Tucker? Are you in there?" An alto voice carried over the purr of the engine.

"I am... yes... just coming..."

Sophie stepped towards the cave mouth. Stopping, she glanced over her shoulder again to Roxie. She couldn't just leave her. Turning, she scuttled past the fire, squeezing between Roxie and the rough cave wall. A thump of rope landed behind her.

"Roxie... I know you're hurting... but I just want to... Oh, Roxie! Your eyes!" She cried out as Roxie shifted her wing, uncovering her slender head.

A sheen of misty white had spread across Roxie's great eyes, criss-crossed with lines of clarity that seemed to ripple as she blinked. Sophie dropped to her knees by Roxie's muzzle, reaching out her hand, then pulling back in hesitation.

"What has happened to her eyes!" She looked up at Drake.

*'That is a sign of extreme pain.'* Drake sighed. *'Our third eyelid locks in place, we don't know why, ...it will ease, she will see again...but it isn't a good sign.'*

Sophie turned back to her friend. She felt the cold trickle of tears over her cheeks.

"Oh Roxie, I'm so sorry..." Carefully, she stretched out her hand, placing it gently on the top of Roxie's long snout. "Thank you. For saving my life, and for all the wonderful things you have done before hand. You are a truly great friend, and anything I can do to help I would..."

Grunting, Roxie lifted her head to align with her own.

"Get well soon!" Sophie flung her arms round the slender neck, pressing her cheek against Roxie's.

"Miss Tucker?" The alto voice repeated, calling her back.

"Coming." Sophie pulled herself away. "I'm so very sorry…Thank you again…. See you soon."

Turning, she slipped back along the cliff wall, hurrying to the cliff mouth under the steady gaze of the red dragon. She paused at the edge, blinking in the sunlight. It felt at odds with the darkness settling around her friend. Staring across the tranquil lake she could almost forget the events of moments ago. Distant bleating of sheep confirmed life was continuing as normal on the mountains beyond the quarry.

"Miss Sophie Tucker?" The alto voice recalled her attention, and she glanced down to see a man standing at the front of a small rubber dinghy, his head in line with her feet. "I'm Detective Inspector Rhys Aneurin. Are you alright?"

"I… yes." Sophie nodded. "Yes I am." She looked down at him, and the companion at the rear who held the motor, keeping the boat against the rock. Stirred by the purring engine, the water lapped at its side.

"Right." The inspector nodded, flicking a glance into the darkness of the cave behind her. "Well, let's get you back to shore and into some dry clothes. That will help…" He indicated a rope ladder that trailed out of the cave. She glanced back as it disappeared into the darkness, noting it pressed to the ground under Drake's hind claw.

*'I won't drop it.'*

"I know." Sophie nodded, flashing him a grin. "I didn't think you would."

*'Why are you sorry?'* Drake tilted his head as he looked down at her.

Puzzled, Sophie hesitated, turning back.

*'Why did you apologise to Roxie? This has nothing to do with you.'*

"Because she's been hurt..."

*'Not because of you. They weren't shooting at you.'*

"Then why?"

*'They used you to expose her. They were targeting Roxie. It could have been anyone they shot down.'*

"Jesus!" Sophie gasped, glancing back at Roxie, fresh tears brimming. "Well I'm sorry that there are people out there who would do that."

"Come along Miss Tucker." The Inspector frowned from below.

Lowering herself to the floor, she grimaced as the jumpsuit clung to her skin. With her feet dangling over the slate, she reached for the rope. She slotted her foot onto the first rung, twisting round and starting her retreat to the boat.

The rope grated against her palms, creaking as it took her weight. Her fingers skimmed against the smooth slate. After a few treads, she felt the Inspectors arm slide up against her own, supporting her. As her feet settled into the dinghy, she turned, following the Inspector as he sank to the seat behind him. The second man leaned forward, offering a thick woollen blanket. She wrapped it round her shoulders with a nod of thanks as he returned to his seat.

The rope ladder jumped away from the slate, tumbling with a thud at their feet. Detective Inspector Aneurin glanced back at the cave briefly, as his colleague revved up the motor.

"So Miss Tucker." He looked back with a serious expression. "Could you tell me what happened here today?"

"I'll certainly try." Sophie hesitated, suddenly aware of what she was facing. She didn't want to betray her friend, but how to explain how she survived such a fall was beyond her. She glanced back at the dark spot on the grey blue cliff behind her.

*'Tell him everything. They're both one of us.'* Drake instructed, appearing in the cave mouth, red scales glinting as he nodded his head.

"We need to get this first interview complete before we return to the cabin where your colleagues are, I think quite understandably, a little shaken." The Inspector prompted.

"Oh, right... ok. Um...It all happened rather quickly I'm afraid...." Sophie spluttered.

"I was the last to go down the wire. I chickened out before then... So I was on, flying... I mean, er... zipping, down over the little wood thing over there... when I suddenly wasn't. I was falling. My head dropped first, so I slid by my feet a bit...Christ..." She paused, bile rising in her stomach as she recalled the sudden lurch and jarring swing over the trees.

"Then I just went. I don't know why...but I was falling. I closed my eyes, couldn't bear to see all that blurring..." The bile churned. Twisting she leaned over the side of the boat as a stream of vomit burned at her throat.

Her face flushed as she felt the steady gaze of the inspector and his colleague on her as she emptied the contents of her stomach into the lake. She could feel herself trembling as she clutched the side of the boat. The hum of the engine stopped. As the boat slowed, drifting on unseen currents, she closed her eyes, waiting for a fresh surge of bile. The gentle lapping of the water and the sweet singing of some distant birds in the rippling foliage seeped into her consciousness. Steadying her breathing, she opened her eyes again. Staring into the lake, she realised her helmet remained in place, pressed against her scalp.

Reaching up, she flicked the clasp free and eased it off as she turned back to the inspector. The breeze skimmed through her hair, teasing the damp strands that clung to her head.

"Sorry about that."

"Don't you worry about it." He held out a handkerchief. "You've had shock. That fall would upset anyone.... But I do need to ask that you complete your story..."

Running the smooth cotton over her lips, Sophie nodded.

"Well... I don't know what to say really. First I was falling, and then I wasn't. Something had my arm. Pulling me upwards. I saw..." She hesitated, looking out across the tranquil quarry. It all seemed so normal.

"You saw what Miss Tucker?"

"I saw a dragon." Turning back, she stared him directly in his eyes. She frowned as she noted a flash of gold spark in his hazel irises. "I saw a dragon. It had me by the arm, and pulled me in to its chest. It hugged me.... She looked at me, reassured me that she had hold of me... showed me her face, that I had nothing to ..."

"She showed you her face?!"

"Yes... well an impression of it... I don't know. It was a fleeting glimpse... then the noise started. Rapid explosions ... gunfire. Took me a moment to realise what it was." Sophie shook her head. "Roxie roared... so loud...I think she must have been hit...Then we were twisting, flying, swooping round the quarry. I couldn't see much, I was pressed close to Roxie... facing into her... Then she said something about being a bit rough and we hit the lake...."

Sophie shivered, recalling the crash that had reverberated through Roxie's body.

"She got me to the surface... I don't know how...I couldn't swim, though I wanted to... my legs were still in the harness...so I clung to her neck and she ... she tried not to sink...I could see she was struggling, but we didn't have far to go... We got to the cliff and she pulled us into the cave... I think that's Drake's, isn't it? He came in, and lit a fire. Roxie's in the corner, she's hurt..." Sophie glanced back. "Is there anything you can..."

"You think I can be of some assistance?!" Detective Inspector Aneurin raised an eyebrow.

"Drake said I could trust you..."

"He told you that?"

"Yes, as we were leaving..." Sophie took a deep breath, scowling at him. "Detective Inspector, I am not imagining it. I know what I saw, what I felt, what I heard. Roxie and Drake are Dragons. She saved my life. I want to do what I can to help her, but I don't know how. I don't want to betray her secret, but Drake tells me you are also a dragon..."

"Did he now?"

"Well, he said you are both one of us..."

Detective Inspector Aneurin shared a glance with his colleague, pausing to study her carefully. Under his austere gaze, Sophie pulled the woollen blanket closer, but sat tall. She would not be intimidated.

"Very well Miss Tucker." The inspector smiled. "Drake is right. Both Noak and I are dragons, and we will do what we can to help your friend. But we are not medics. Dragons are tough Miss Tucker, particularly one as old as Roxie. I do not doubt that she needs assistance, and can assure you that is on route, but Drake has assured me that there is no immediate threat to life."

"Her eyes... he said it wasn't a good sign!"

"They are indicators of pain, certainly... and after receiving a volley of machine gunfire I don't wonder that she is in pain...but dragon hide is tough, and I believe that no internal damage is done..."

"But all that blood...!"

"As I say Miss Tucker, I cannot assist with that. Help is on the way, but they have further to travel and will arrive by night fall." Detective Inspector Aneurin smiled reassuringly. "My job, is to try and ensure that this situation does not become public knowledge."

"As today has demonstrated, we dragons cannot risk exposure. We are a threatened species that can only survive if we adapt to live alongside humans. To do that, we must remain a secret. That is my job, and today it will be a challenge." He flashed a glance at Noak at the motor and the engine roared into life.

"You are not at risk from me, I promise you that." Sophie determined.

"I am very pleased to hear it Miss Tucker." Detective Inspector Aneurin smiled. "However, I am less confident about your colleagues... would you have any idea how much they saw?"

"None at all, I'm sorry... they would all have been at the end of the zip wire, probably watching and waiting for me...with Roxie probably... beyond that I can't guess." Sophie shook her head. "But I don't think that there will be any trouble. They all love Roxie..."

Detective Inspector Aneurin and Noak exchanged glances, but remained silent as they approached the lakeside. A police Landover waited by the waters edge. Cutting the engine, Noak guided the boat into the shallows. Jumping over the side, he landed with a splash, and pulled the dinghy up until it grated to a halt on the beach.

Satisfied it was firmly on the ground, he waded up to Sophie, offering her his hand to assist her out of the dinghy. She accepted with a grateful smile, wobbling as she straddled the side. Detective Inspector Aneurin opened the car door for her. She pulled herself in, leaning back into the comforting padding with a sigh. Clicking her seatbelt into place, she closed her eyes. She ignored the trickle of water from her hair down her spine. The car rocked as the doors slammed behind the police men, before the engine rumbled into life.

They jolted up the road for only a few moments, before stopping before the cabin. As she got out, the sound of raised voices drifted from the timber building. Detective Inspector Aneurin raised an eyebrow at her briefly before he pushed the door open.

"Good afternoon ladies and Gentlemen." He bellowed, slicing through the melee. "I'm Detective Inspector Aneurin..."

"Sophie!"

"Oh my God, Sophie, are you alright?!"

"She's alive!"

Sophie gaped as a swarm of people rushed up to her, pushing past the inspector who scowled. She was pulled forward into a firm hug, buried in Mike's chest as others gushed their astonishment. Pulling herself free from Mike, she was instantly pulled against Mary, while Paula clasped her hand.

"Are you alright?!"

"Yes... yes I'm fine!"

"Christ, even after all that...after ..."

"If everyone would just return to their seats and give Miss Tucker some room..." Detective Inspector Aneurin boomed. "As I was saying, I'm Detective Inspector Aneurin and I'm here to find out exactly what happened this afternoon."

"What happened?!" Mike snorted. "I'll tell you what happened... Sophie was shot at and our boss turned into a monster!"

"She saved Sophie!" Paula objected.

"And that makes her less of a monster?" Mike sneered.

"She's a dragon for pete's sake, of course she's a monster." Justine exclaimed, turning to Sophie. "What did she do to you?"

"What?" Sophie was startled.

"What did she do to you?"

"Nothing... I mean she caught me, saved me..." Sophie shook her head, puzzled. "What else would she do? Why would she?"

"She's a dragon Sophie! It's what they do."

"What is what they do Justine?" Paula asked, crossing her arms. "Go on. Tell us. From all your experience..."

"Well, they..."

"Does it matter that we don't know?" Mike snarled. "They are vicious monsters!"

"You think Roxie is vicious?!" Sophie exclaimed. "Our Roxie? Generous, kind hearted, giving Roxie? Ridiculous!"

"She's a walking weapon. Of course she's vicious." Simon interjected.

"A walking weapon?!"

"Did you see her teeth?! Those claws?! And lets not forget the fire..."

"Of course I saw those claws Justine. I was in them." Sophie stood. "But Roxie is no more of a threat than I am. All dogs have teeth, but they don't use them on us! So what if Roxie has them too?

"Those men shooting at her today were far more vicious than she is. Those men who were using a weapon that humans have developed for the exclusive purpose of destroying each other. Where are those men Inspector?" She turned to Detective Inspector Aneurin.

"They are currently under arrest awaiting interview." He responded non-committedly.

"So, those men who were shooting at us, at me, have faced dragons and are still alive. Roxie, who chose to save me from them is currently lying critically wounded, alone. And you tell me that she is the monster?" Sophie snorted.

"But…"

"Faced what dragons…"

"Other dragons…?"

"Christ! Will you listen to yourselves! I thought that we worked for a company that prizes diversity and respect? I thought we prided ourselves on our non-judgemental policies?"

"But she's a bloody dragon, Sophie! A Dragon!" Mike barked.

"And why are you all afraid of dragons?" Drake asked, his deep voice carried through from the changing area. Sophie glanced over with a smile, noting the black jumpsuit hanging open at his waist.

"Because the medieval monks who last discovered us say that you should be? When did you last believe everything that the medieval world told you? Do you still believe the world is flat? Is your health care system based on a balance of four humours ruled by the planets? No. So why should you be afraid of dragons? Hell, you've killed more of us, more of yourselves then we ever could!"

Sophie noted Detective Inspector Aneurin glare at Drake, who shrugged. The team muttered amongst themselves, exchanging worried glances. Some shuffled back from Drake, but Sophie could see that Drake's words had touched nerves.

"How long have we worked for Roxie?" Sophie pressed. "Ruth, you've been with her the longest, what 15 years now? Have you ever seen her hurt anyone?"

Sniffing, Ruth shook her head.

"Paul, James, Andrea? Sure, she's got a temper, yes I've seen her smash a plate or two, but she's never aimed anything at anyone of us. She listens to us, gives us time when we need it, and tolerates our arguments.

"Mike, you know she stands up for you when you clients are demanding the ridiculous. Justine, she devoted time and money to you when Paul pushed you to the edge, drove you to the extreme. Sure she will defend others from you both when she sees you over step the mark, but she's never cruel when she does. Is she?" She demanded. "Is she?!"

Shaking their heads, they scowled at each other as they sank to their seats.

"But how can we trust her when she has been keeping such a secret…" Andrea countered. "When she has been hiding her true…"

"Hiding a truth that could kill her?" Sophie asked. "Yes, it could kill her… that's what those men were trying to do. Of course she's going to keep her identity a secret. And listen to us, I bet you've already discussed what to do about her…" She glared round the room, noting the uncomfortable shuffling amidst the group.

"And come on, who in truth doesn't have a secret? I know I do. None of you here know that I am a claustrophobic Lesbian who is allergic to olives.

"You don't know, because it was never relevant for you to know, it never came up in conversation and I saw no need to announce it. But Roxie knows. We discussed it in my first appraisal, and it's never come up since."

"That's all well and good Sophie…" Andrea sniffed. "But your secret can't kill us."

"Christ, do you not listen?! Roxie's secret didn't kill me today, it nearly killed her! It hasn't killed us while she kept it, and it won't kill us now we know…"

Sophie sighed. She looked round for a chair. Clarissa smiled at her, pushing forward her own padded office chair. Grateful, Sophie sank onto the seat. Closing her eyes she leaned back, pulling the blanket round her. The wool grated on her trembling fingers.

She listened to the rapid beating of her own heart, as her team shuffled and muttered amongst themselves. Tears dampened her eyelashes. The harsh judgements of her colleagues had taken her by surprise. She was saddened by the fear, distrust and lack of memory they had displayed.

"Well, who'd have thought it would take a near death plunge to make timid little Sophie so talkative?" Simon spoke near by. She could hear the smile in his voice, and opened her eyes to find him crouching by her side.

"You're right of course. As usual." He nodded. "It's just been a bit of a shock…"

"You had a bit of a shock?" She snorted. "Try plunging head first into a quarry to be caught by a mythical beast!"

"Alright, alright. You win… You're right…again!" He chuckled, shaking his head. "But we aren't all as adaptable as you." He looked across the room to where Mike and Justine were eyeing Drake warily. "Give us time."

"I can do that… but I'm not sure time is something that others can spare… they need certainty, confidence that secrets will be honoured." Sophie looked across to Detective Inspector Aneurin who was watching the group carefully. "It isn't just Roxie who is endangered by exposure…" She paused to sneeze.

"Christ, look at you! You're all wet and here we are chatting like God knows what…" Simon looked up. "We need to get you warm and into some dry clothes… Just wait here."

Sophie watched him push through the group that filled the small room. He dipped his head to Drake, shifting uncomfortably, and not quite meeting his eyes. She noted Drake glance up at her, wide eyed, nodding a murmuring his ascent to Simon. With a jerk of his head he signalled for her to come to the changing area.

As she eased her way through the group, she felt their lingering touch as they squeezed her arm, her hands. Murmuring their encouragement as she passed.

"Well said Sophie."

"You're so right."

"How could we forget Roxie…"

"You'll need a fresh set of clothes." Drake sniffed, smiling down at her. "Help yourself to a jump suit. Clarissa will show you where the toilets are so you can change in a bit of privacy."

"Thank you." She smiled as he stepped aside.

"No, thank you…" He placed a hand on her shoulder. "It's been a long time since anyone has stood up for us like that…"

"Alright, ladies and gentleman…" Detective Inspector Aneurin sniffed. "Can I please get back to business… I need to take statements from all of you."

Rustling through the suits, Sophie paused as a door opened by her side. Clarissa stood with a steaming mug.

"I thought you might need this"

"Oooh, yes. Thanks." Sophie closed her fingers round the proffered mug.

Ignoring the sting of heat on her palm, she lifted the mug to her lips. The steam enveloped her nose, spreading warmth across she cheeks.

"You hang on to that, I'll find you a suit. What size?"

"Oh, erm… I think this one is a medium."

"Cool."

Sophie sipped at the dark tea, watching Clarissa cross efficiently to a section of railings and rifling through the hanging fabric. "Here we go. Follow me, the best place to change is back here."

Sophie followed Clarissa back through the door and she found herself in a room filed with filing cabinets, desks and walls clad with paper, showing climate graphs, maps and stunning pictures of the Snowdonian landscapes. Clarissa opened another door, stepping aside and ushering Sophie into an empty room.

"The boys tend to forget that we have this place. We haven't quite figured out what to use it for, so at the moment it is a great place to change..." Clarissa glanced over to a neat pile of clothes and rucksack in the corner. "I use it when I cycle in."

"Thanks."

"Take your time." Clarissa retreated.

Leaving the tea on the windowsill to cool down, Sophie quickly peeled her wet clothes off her body. Using the blanket as a towel, she rubbed the lingering water from her skin. Warm and rosy, she dropped the now damp blanket to one side and reached for the jumpsuit. The fabric was a soothing contrast to the blanket.

Refreshed, she collected her cup, gathered her wet clothes in the blanket, clutching it under her arm as she returned through the office to the team. She watched as Detective Inspector Aneurin, Noak and a female colleague worked their way round the room, taking notes in quiet discussion with individual team members. With a yawn, she leaned against the doorframe, and turned her attention to the tranquil sky visible through the cabin window.

"Alright. Many thanks for your time." Detective Inspector Aneurin stepped back. "Your statements are much appreciated. However, I would like to re-confirm everything that your friend Miss Tucker said earlier. It is essential for everyone that this story remains untold. Today's event is contained with the quarry.

"You are all sensible people, your company's reputation for respect and judgement free treatment is well known, and in its turn respected. For the company to continue, the secret now revealed must remain yours...."

"Is that a threat?" Mike bristled.

"Not at all sir." Detective Inspector Aneurin shook his head. "It is a fact. Roxie will move on, will sell or simply close down the company that you have all worked so hard to build. Her survival drive will require her to relocate. If she is threatened in any way this will be the outcome.

"But beyond that, the lives of many hundreds of dragons are within your hands. If you reveal us to the world, and the world believes you, many more attacks will take place."

"You can't possibly know that..."

"I'm sorry to say, sir, that I do. It has happened before and will happen again... only it will be much easier for people to achieve our extinction now than it ever was in the past. We are not the invincible creatures that history believes us to be.

"So I ask that you forget about us. But, I know that today's event is remarkable, and will be deeply imbedded in your memories. So instead, I ask that you accept us. That you respect us and you protect us. I can do no more than that."

"And if we don't?" Justine sneered. "What will you do then?"

"I can't say, because I don't know. If you are believed..." He paused to look round. "...you will be a threat to us. But we have survived many threats. We relocate, we adapt, we hide if necessary. That is our secret to survival, and it doesn't matter that you know it, because you cannot counter it.

"But I would re-iterate, if you wish to retain your jobs, Roxie's secret, our privacy, is paramount." With a nod, and a smile to Sophie, Detective Inspector Aneurin turned. Followed by Noak and his colleague, he stepped through the doors. The team stared after them in silence.

---

Roxie stared at the door. Her heart raced, and she could feel tears brimming by her eyelashes. The box lid rattled as she hesitated, shaken by the tremors that shivered down her spine. She didn't want to do this, hated having to face this again.

Taking a deep breath, she stepped forward. The doors slid open, whooshing their welcome as she entered the cool shelter of the hallway. She nodded at the receptionists, who gave her a funny glance as she crossed the crisp marble, to the lift. The button pinged as she called, triggering the gentle hum of motor.

She stepped forward as the doors whisked open, turning to press the button to the fourth floor with her elbow. A dragon spread its wings over the button, confirming the location of the Dragon Design office. Her logo. Her office. Turning away she stared at the silver walls as the lift raced upwards. It wouldn't be hers for much longer.

As the lift slowed to a halt, she took a deep breath. This was the moment that she had been dreading. She had come on a Saturday so that she didn't have to face anyone, but she knew that the desks would remind her of each of her colleagues. Remind her of the family that she would have to leave. Each member with their own signature emblazoned across the desk. Sophie's neat piles; Mike's chaotic spread of papers; Justine's plants over shadowing her telephone and keyboard. Each desk enough to bring the individual to mind as she past.

The doors whipped open and she stepped out into the office. A burst of applause rippled through the space. Astonished, she turned. She stared open mouthed as the team pushed themselves back from their desks. Sophie rushed forward arms wide. She pulled the box from Roxie's arms, throwing it to the floor as she wrapped herself around Roxie's shoulders.

"You don't need that... Surely you know that everyone is welcome here?"